My Grandma Could do ANYTHING in NEW YORK CITY!

by Ric Dilz

RICDesign LLC

Boulder, Colorado

Illustration by Nancy Maysmith and Ric Dilz

My Grandma
could do
ANYTHING...

My Grandma
doesn't bungee jump
from the
Brooklyn Bridge...

But she could!

My Grandma
doesn't skateboard in
Central Park...

But she could!

My Grandma
doesn't dance
in the ballet...

But she could!

My Grandma
doesn't brush dinosaur
teeth at the Museum
of Natural History...

But she could!

My Grandma
doesn't fly a helicopter
around the Empire State
Building...

But she could!

My Grandma
doesn't
ice skate at
Rockefeller Center...

But she could!

My Grandma
doesn't drive a taxi...

But she could!

My Grandma
doesn't direct traffic at
Times Square...

But she could!

My Grandma
doesn't conduct a
subway train...

But she could!

My Grandma
doesn't perform
on Broadway...

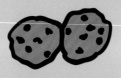

But she could!

My Grandma
doesn't parachute to
the Statue of Liberty...

But she could!

My Grandma
doesn't drive a
horse drawn carriage...

But she could!

I'd rather be horsing around with my Grandchild.
How much do we tip a grandma?
We don't, we just have to look at photos of her grandchild.
Howdy "Neigh"-bor.

My Grandma
could do lots of things,
but I'm so happy with
the one thing she does
the best...

Love Me!

WHAT DO YOU THINK?

SHOUT IT OUT!

THAT'S A FACT, JACK! **OR** GET OUTTA HERE!
(TRUE)   (FALSE)

1 **The Statue of Liberty gets a haircut every three weeks.**

I wonder if she gets a treat afterwards.

2 **The American Museum of Natural History has more dinosaur fossils than any other museum in the world.**

I'm glad those dinosaurs finally found a home!

3 **Horses in Central Park take the subway to work.**

The cabs must be too small for them!

4 **The Rockefeller Christmas Tree is always over 65 feet tall.**

That's like 14 Grandmas standing on each others' shoulders!

5 **Dogs in New York City are so happy, they whistle instead of bark.**

They must smile more, too!

6 New York City cabs are yellow because it makes them easier to see.

 I think pink polka dots would have worked too!

7 The Statue of Liberty's nose is 4½ feet tall.

 Someday you'll be as tall as her nose!

8 The first New York City cab was a dinosaur with a comfy saddle.

 I hope they had a car seat!

9 May 12th in New York City is "Put Your Pants on Your Head" Day.

 Does that mean I put my hat on my feet?

10 The rivers around New York City are made of pudding.

 Chocolate, I hope!

11 Asian elephants at the Bronx Zoo flap their ears to stay cool.

 I wonder if they wag their tails to stay warm!

12 Hot dog vendors in New York City always keep extra mustard in their sneakers.

 They keep their buns in the sun for fun!

13 New York City is called "The Big Apple."

 Are subways the worms in the apple?

ANSWER KEY: 1. F, 2. T, 3. F, 4. T, 5. F, 6. T, 7. T, 8. F, 9. F, 10. F, 11. T, 12. F, 13. T.

Visit www.reindesigns.com
for more fun products!

Author Ric Dilz was born and raised in Schenectady, NY. He is married and has two kids. Ric has always been a big fan of grandmas and New York City! *My Grandma Could Do Anything in New York City* is the 5th book in the *My Grandma Could Do Anything* series.

Published by Rein Designs, Inc.
Boulder, Colorado

ISBN: 9780985968403

Library of Congress Control Nunber: 2012914449

Printed in China.